BENJAMIN
BEAR

IN

BRIGHT IDEAS!

PHILIPPE COUDRAY

BENJAMIN BEAR

IN
BRIGHT IDEAS!

A TOON BOOK BY
PHILIPPE COUDRAY

TOON BOOKS IS AN IMPRINT OF CANDLEWICK PRESS

For my godson, Nicolas

Editorial Director: FRANÇOISE MOULY

Book Design: FRANÇOISE MOULY & JONATHAN BENNETT

Translation: LEIGH STEIN

PHILIPPE COUDRAY'S artwork was drawn in india ink and colored digitally.

Library of Congress Cataloging-in-Publication Data:
Coudray, Philippe.
Benjamin Bear in "Bright ideas!" : a TOON book / by Philippe Coudray.
 p. cm.
 Summary: Benjamin Bear, accompanied by his faithful rabbit friend, continues to share his observations and questions about the world around him.
ISBN 978-1-935179-22-1
1. Graphic novels. [1. Graphic novels. 2. Bears–Fiction. 3. Humorous stories.] I. Title. II. Title: Bright ideas!
PZ7.7.C68Bd 2013
741.5'973–dc23   2012022895

ISBN 13: 978-1-935179-22-1 ISBN 10: 1-935179-22-5

13 14 15 16 17 18 TPN 10 9 8 7 6 5 4 3 2 1

Treetop

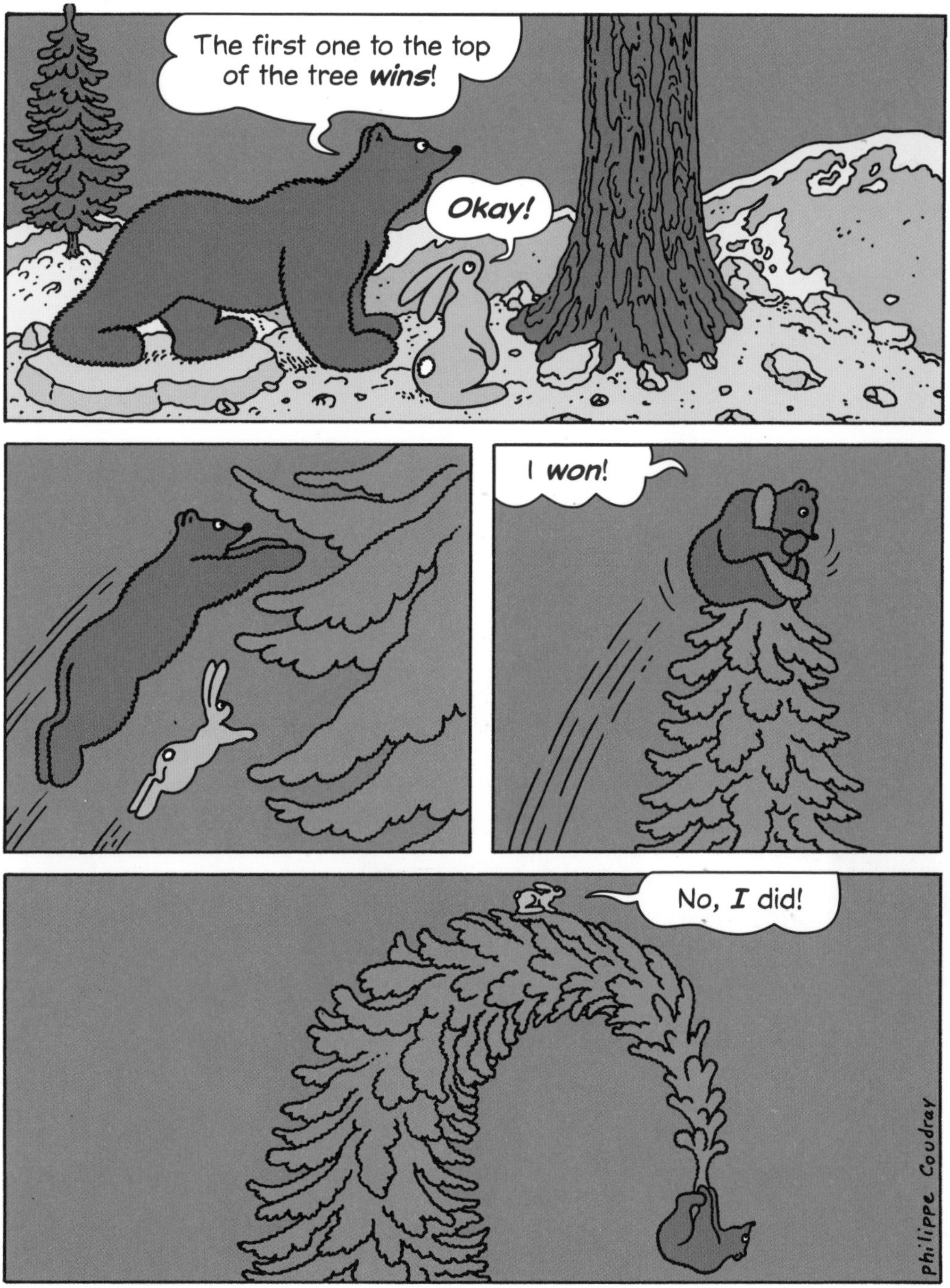

The first one to the top of the tree ***wins***!
Okay!
I ***won***!
No, ***I*** did!
philippe Coudray

Good catch

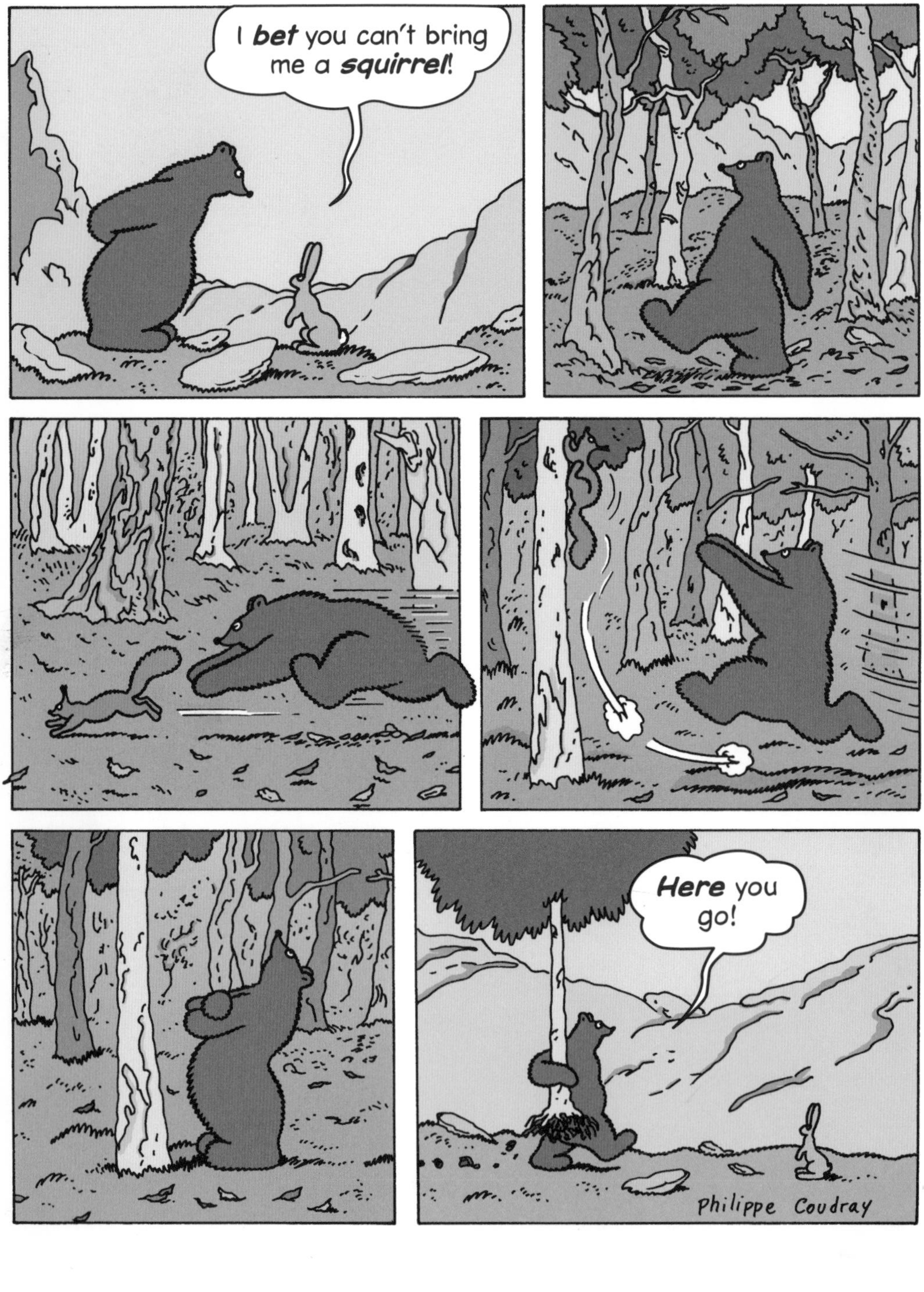

I **bet** you can't bring me a **squirrel**!
Here you go!
Philippe Coudray

Crossing

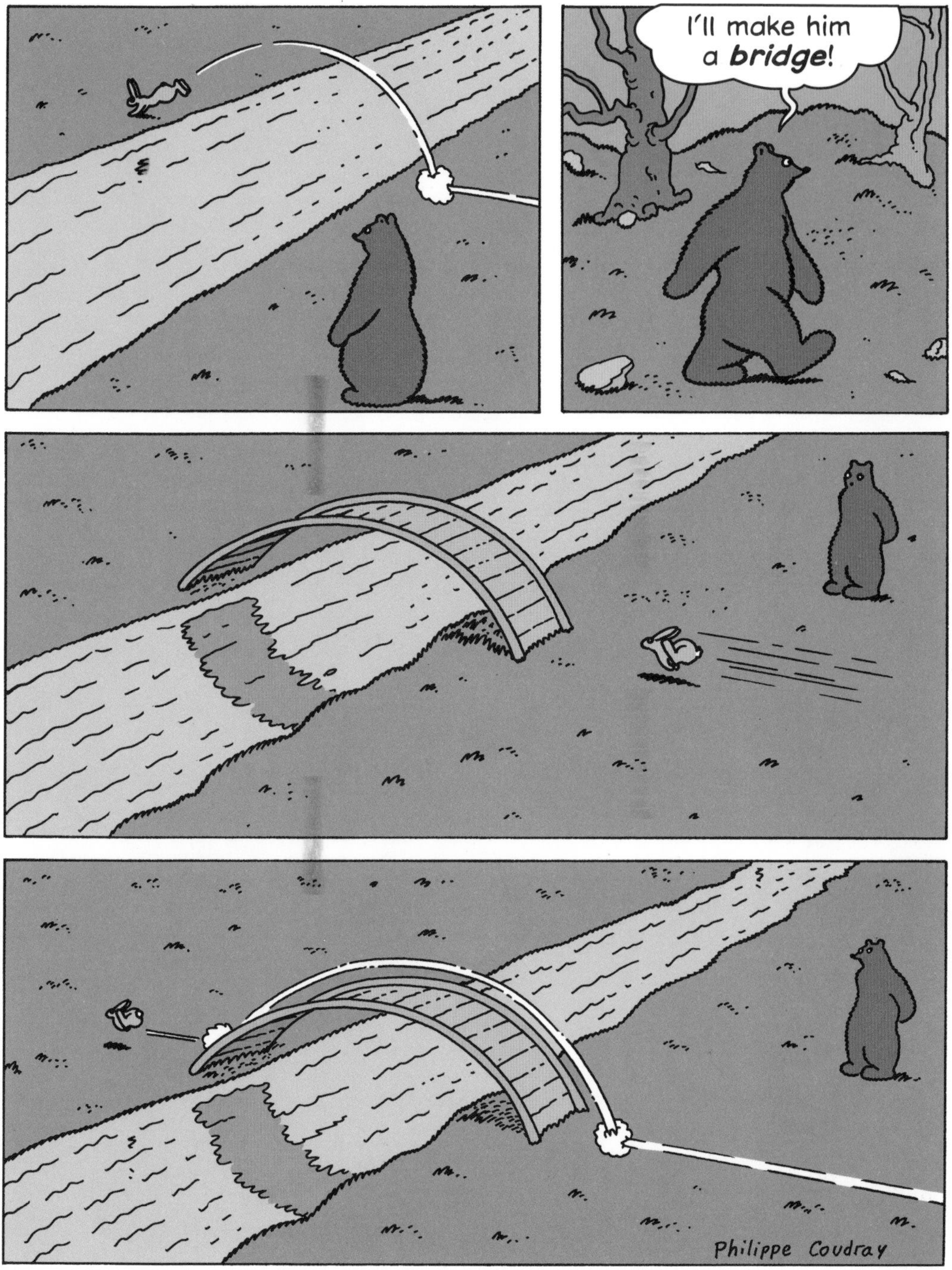
I'll make him a ***bridge***!
Philippe Coudray

Can I get a ride?

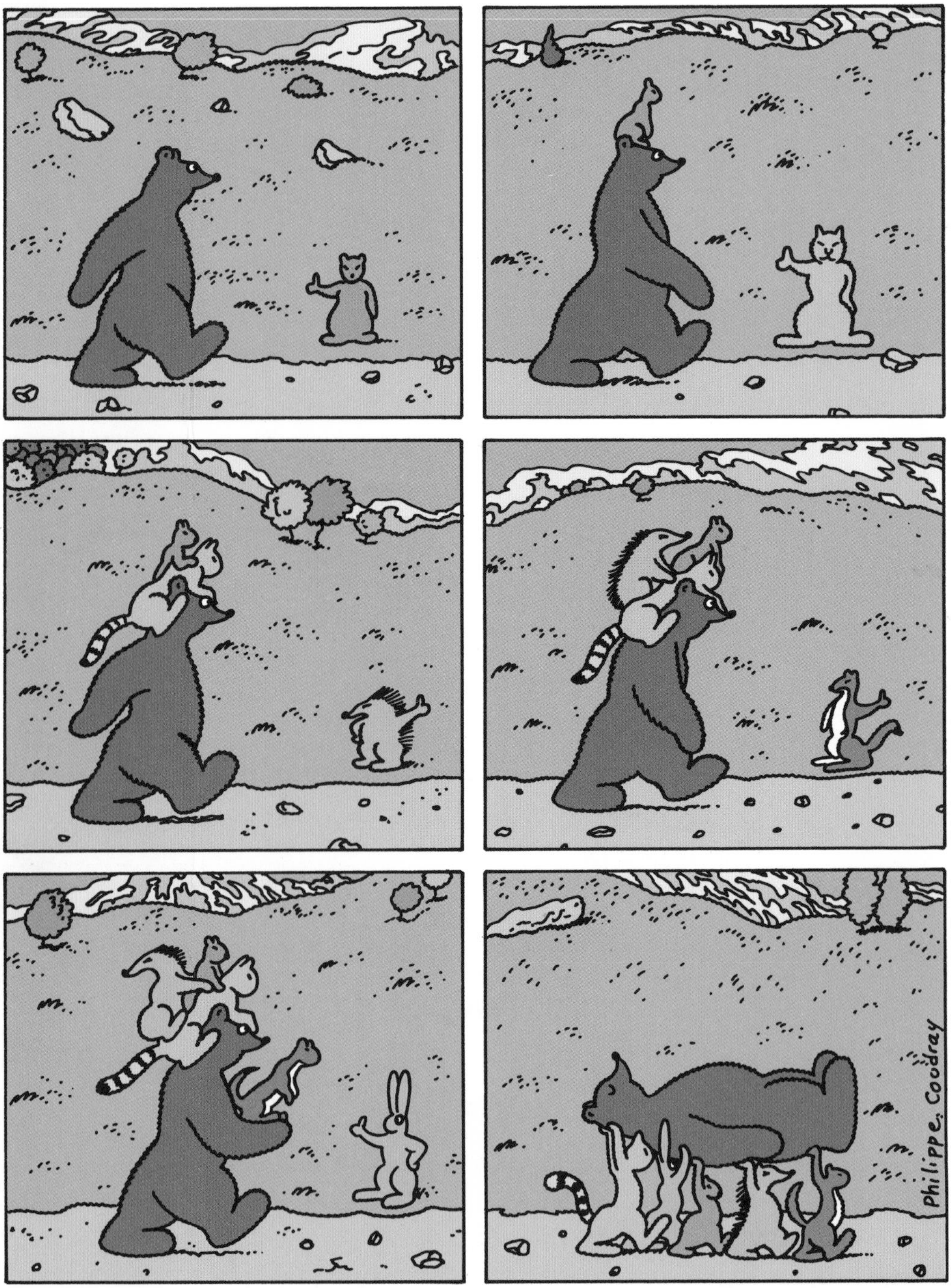
Philippe Coudray

The ladder

Philippe Coudray

11

High wire

I **BET** you can't cross on this wire.
Yes I *can*!
Philippe Coudray

Like a fish to water

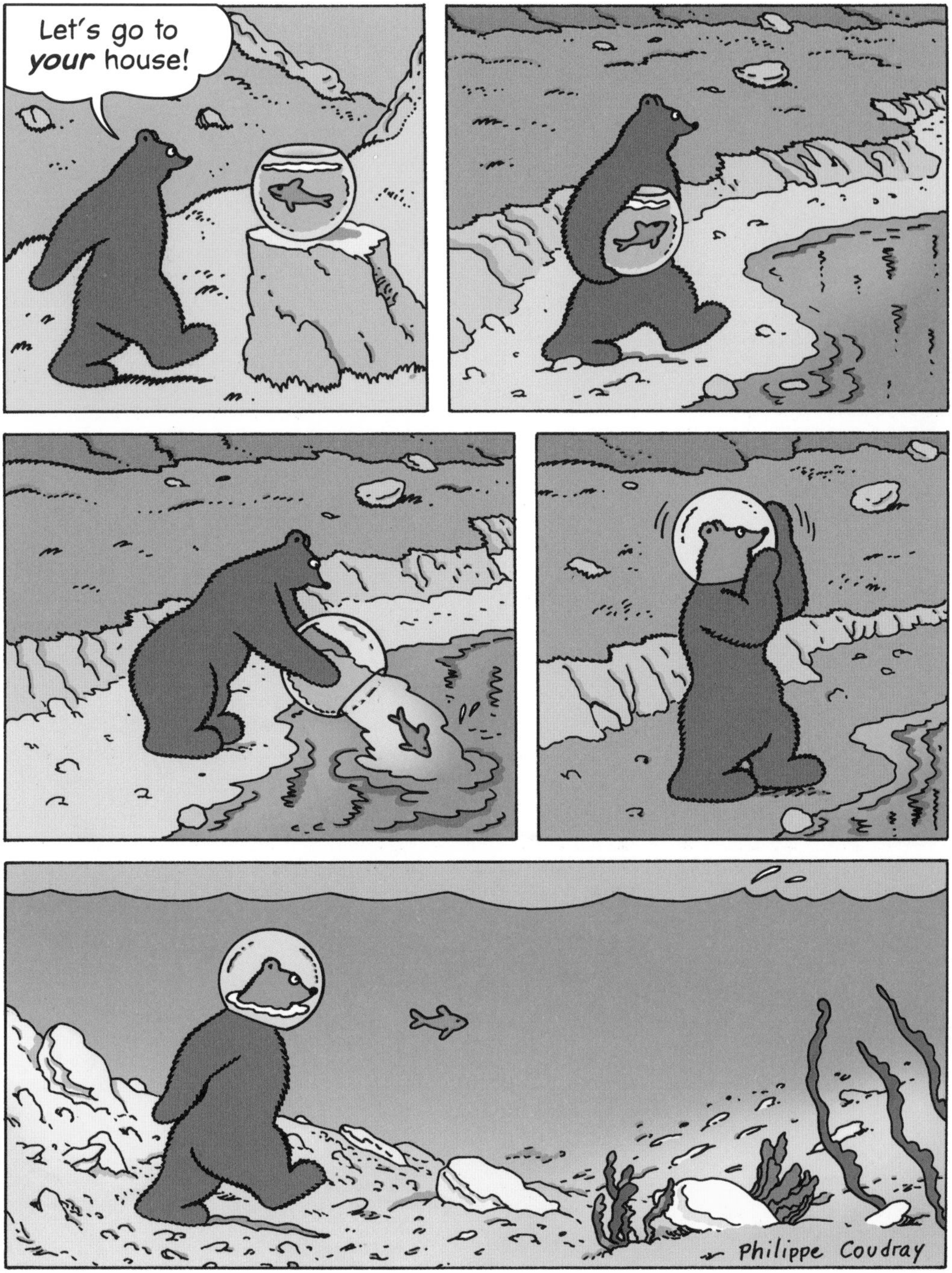

Let's go to ***your*** house!
Philippe Coudray

Keep going

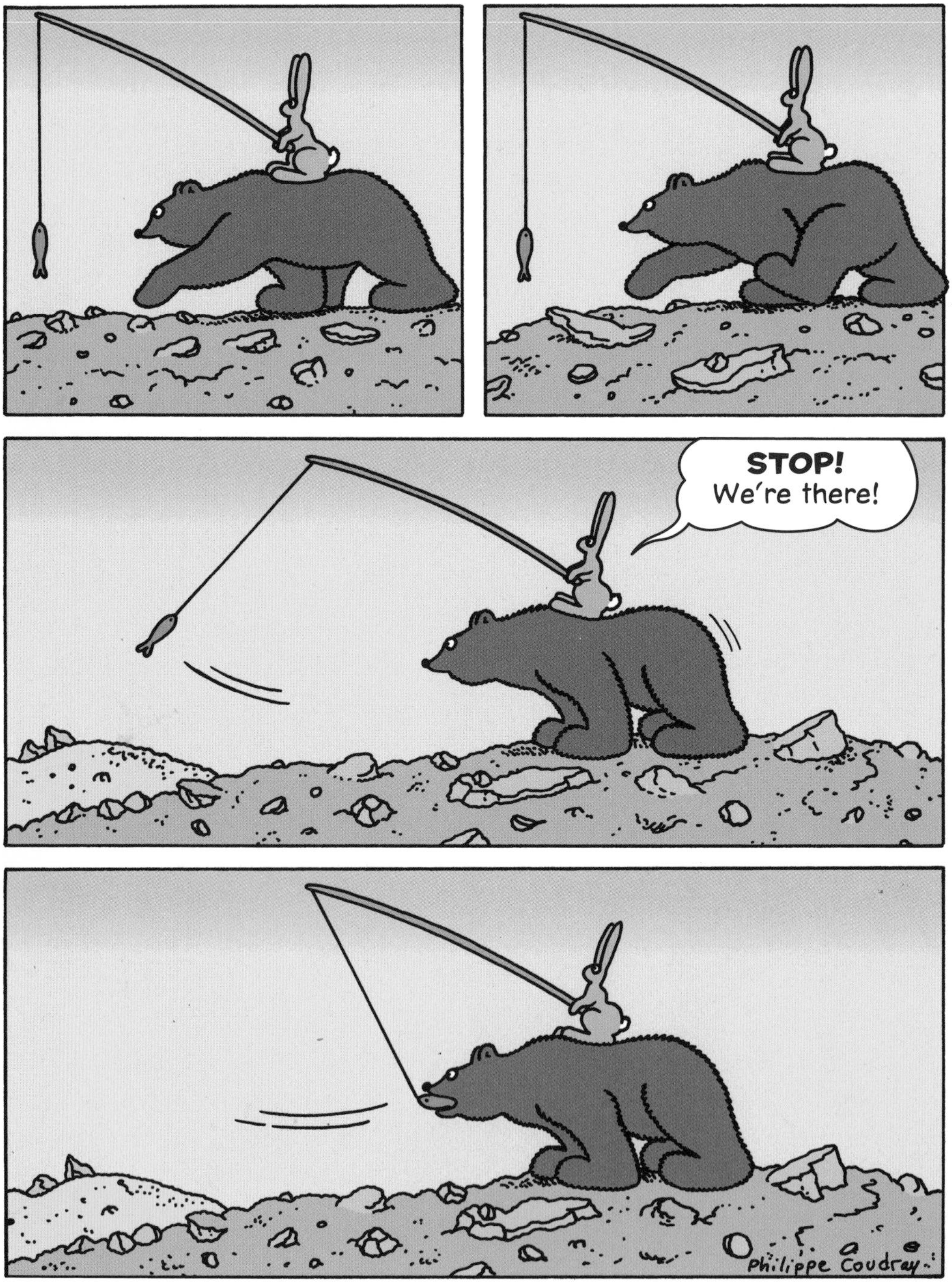
STOP!
We're there!
Philippe Coudray

Follow the leader

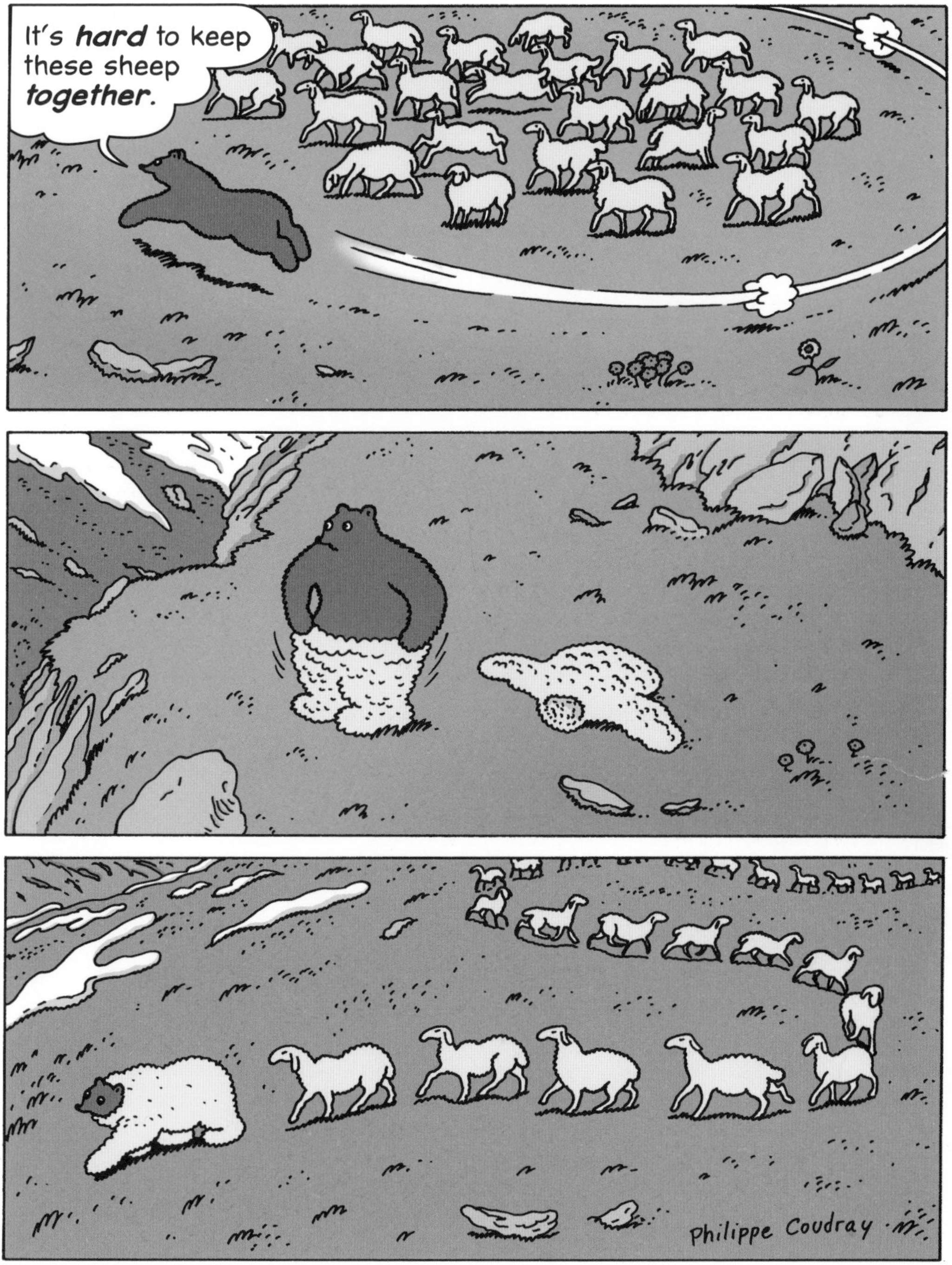

It's *hard* to keep these sheep *together*.
Philippe Coudray

Hot and cold

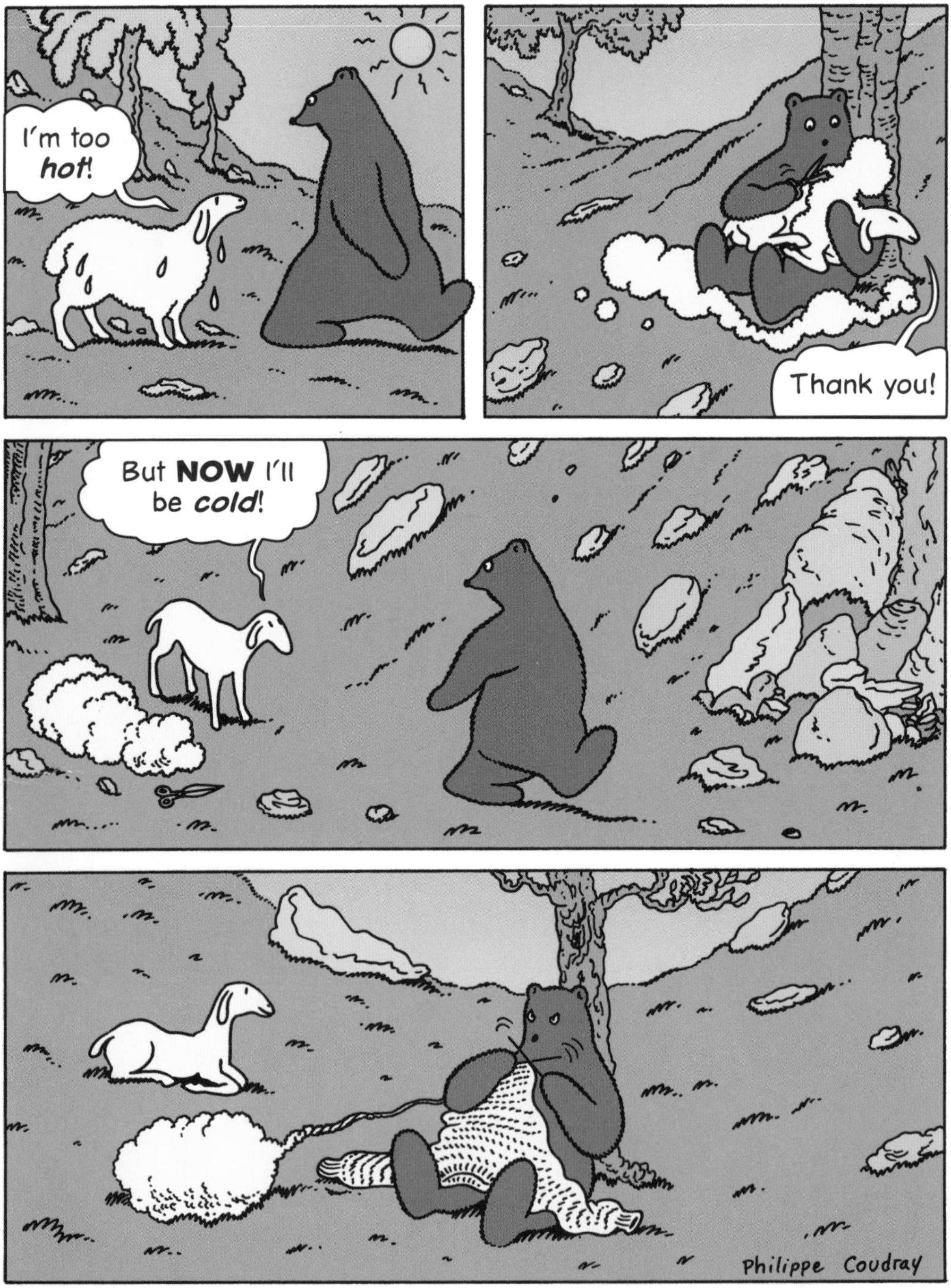

I'm too *hot*!
Thank you!
But **NOW** I'll be *cold*!
Philippe Coudray

Spring cleaning

Philippe Coudray

Stay close

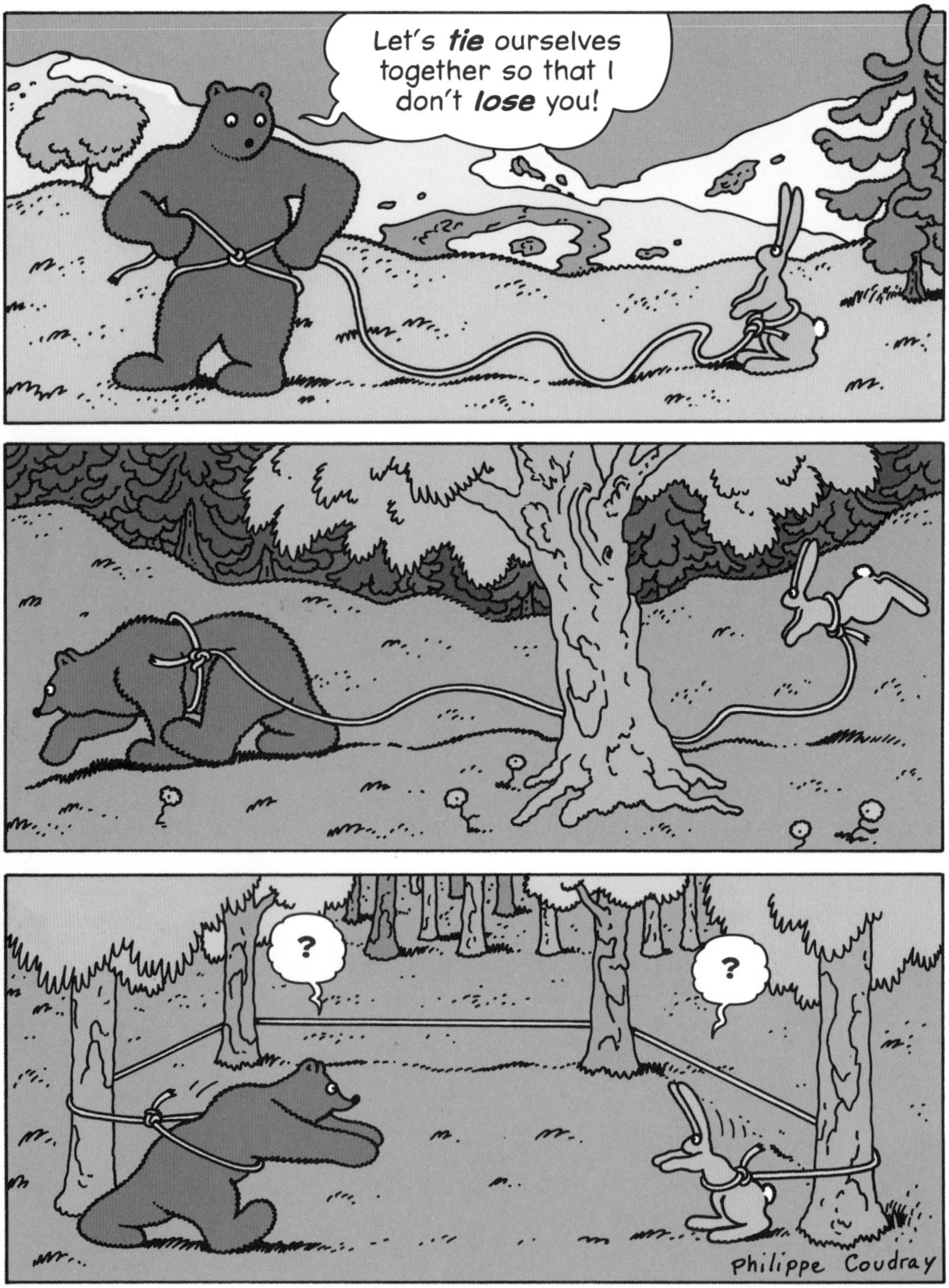
Let's *tie* ourselves together so that I don't *lose* you!
?
?
Philippe Coudray

Something out of nothing

It's impossible to make **something** out of nothing.

One thing, yes! But **two** things, no!

Look. Here's **nothing**...

...and **now**, there are **TWO** things!

Philippe Coudray

It's raining...

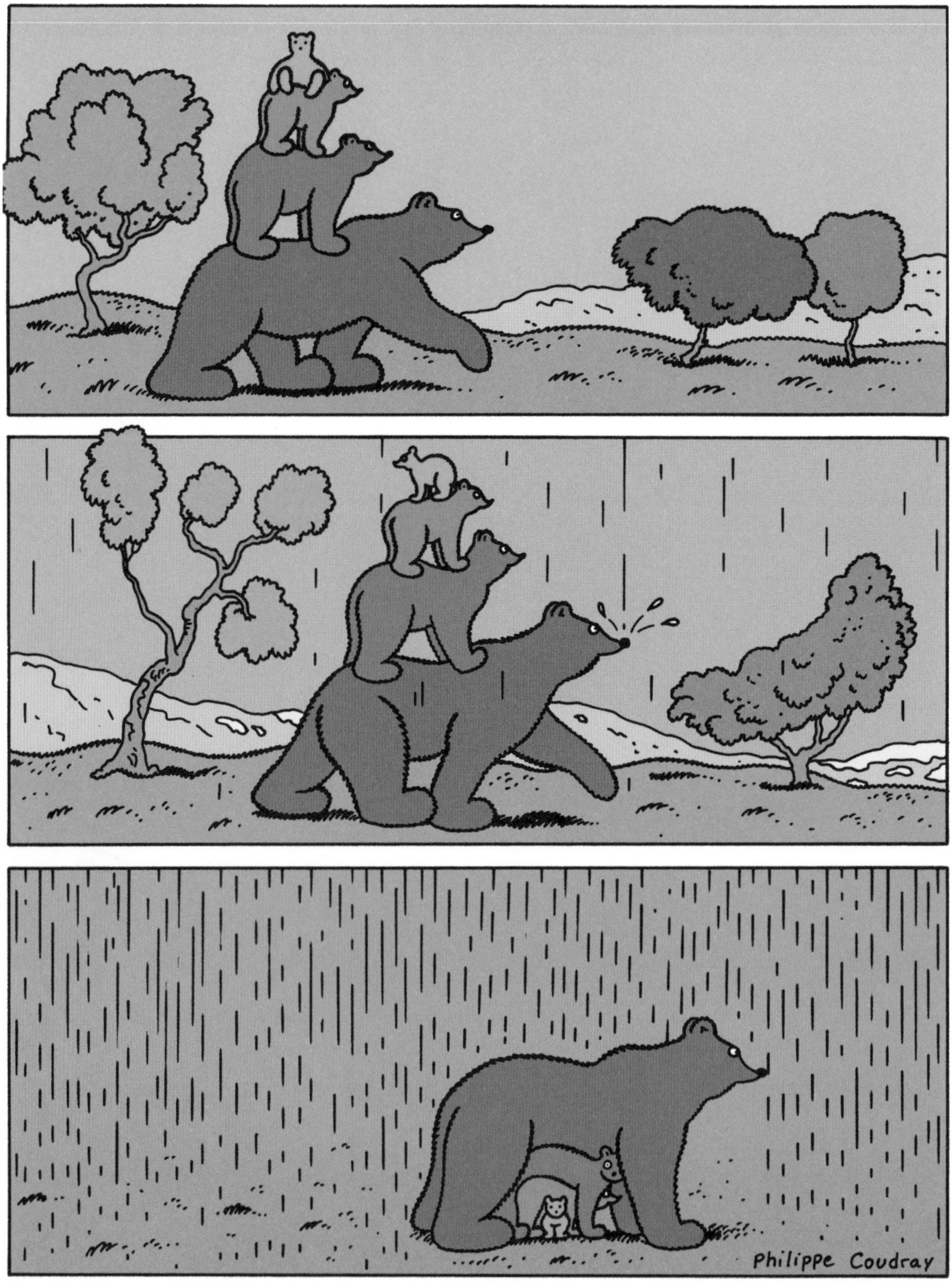
Philippe Coudray

Portrait

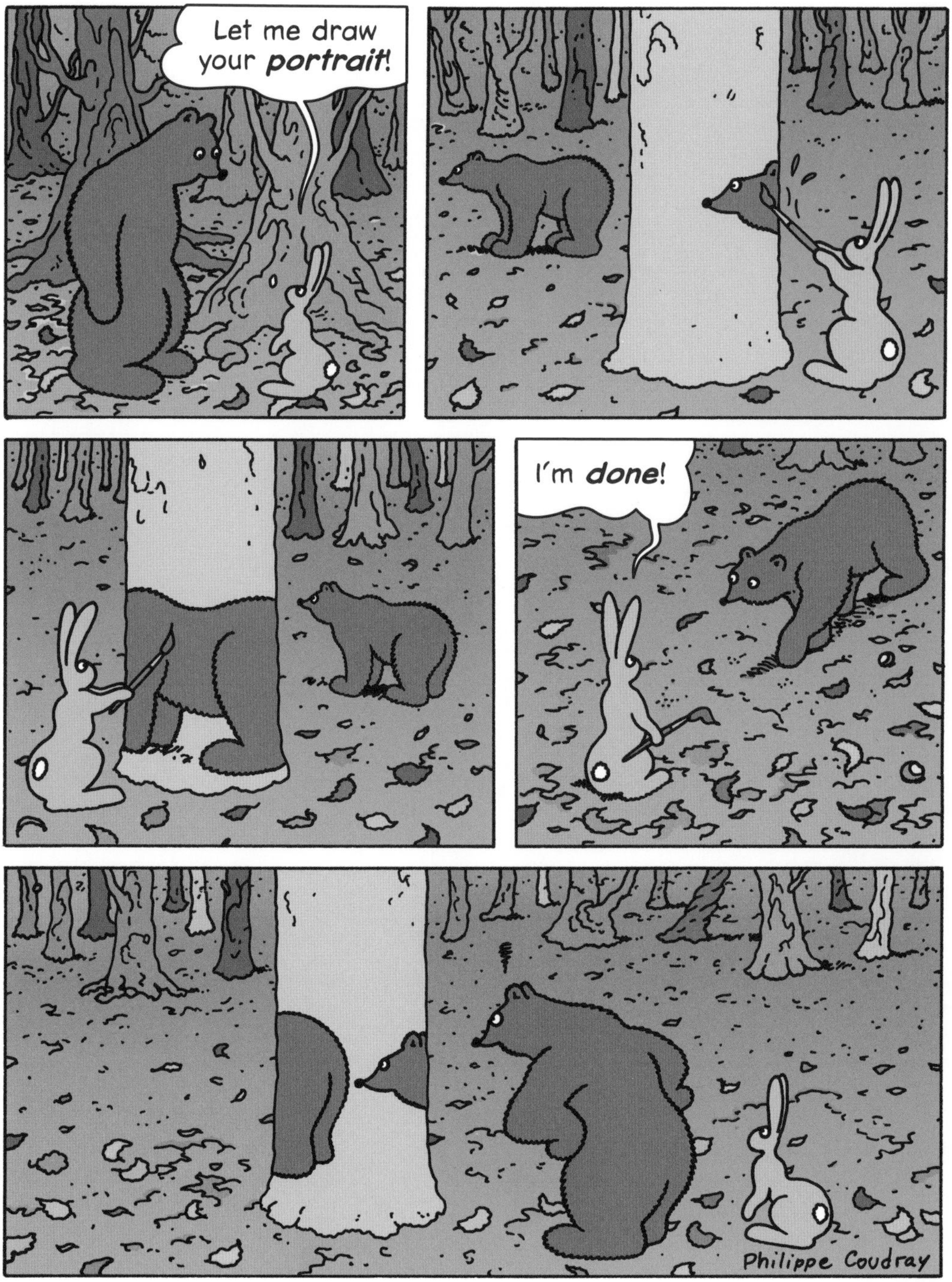
Let me draw your ***portrait***!
I'm ***done***!
Philippe Coudray

A good night's sleep

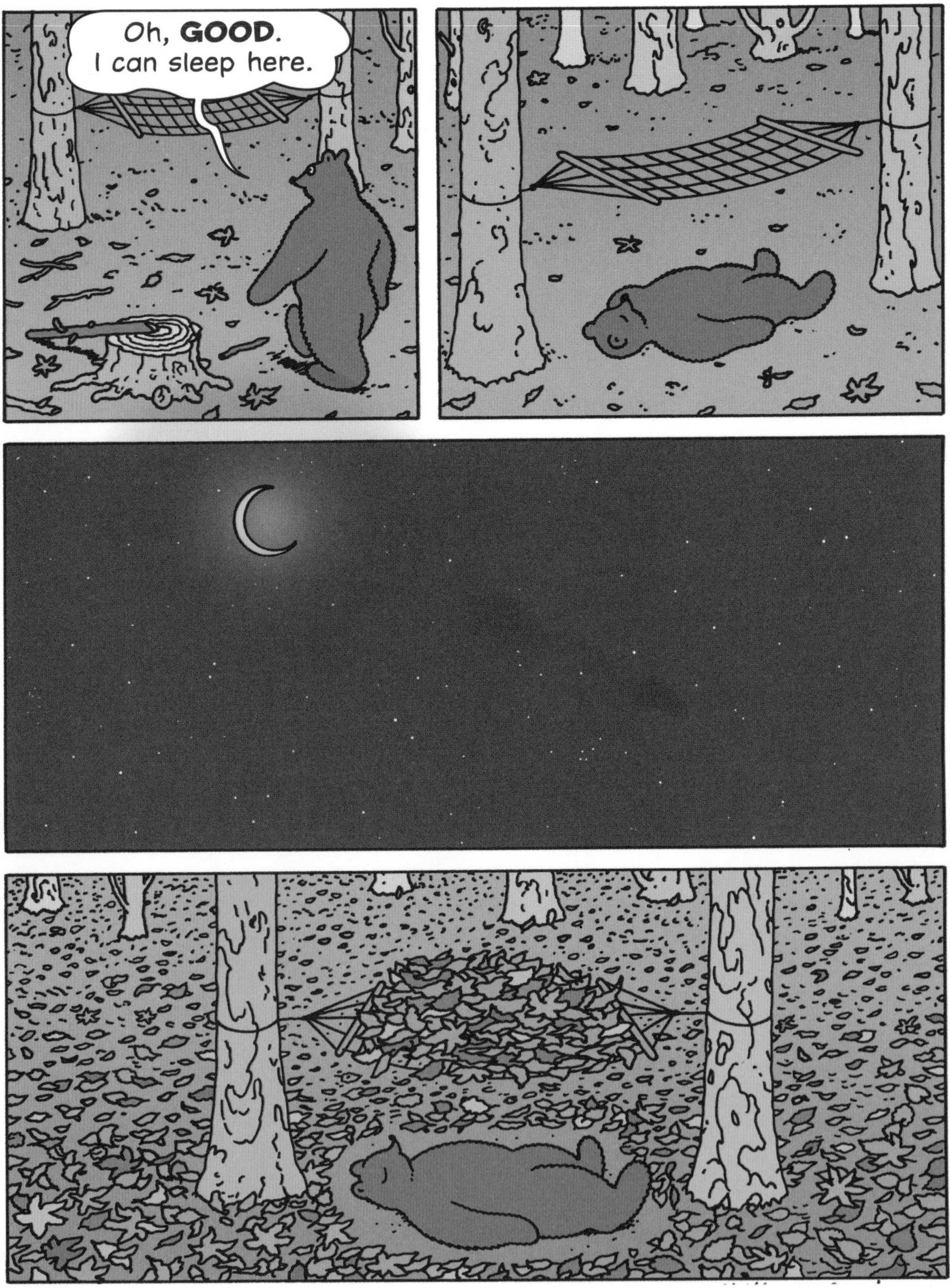
Oh, **GOOD**.
I can sleep here.

Two for one

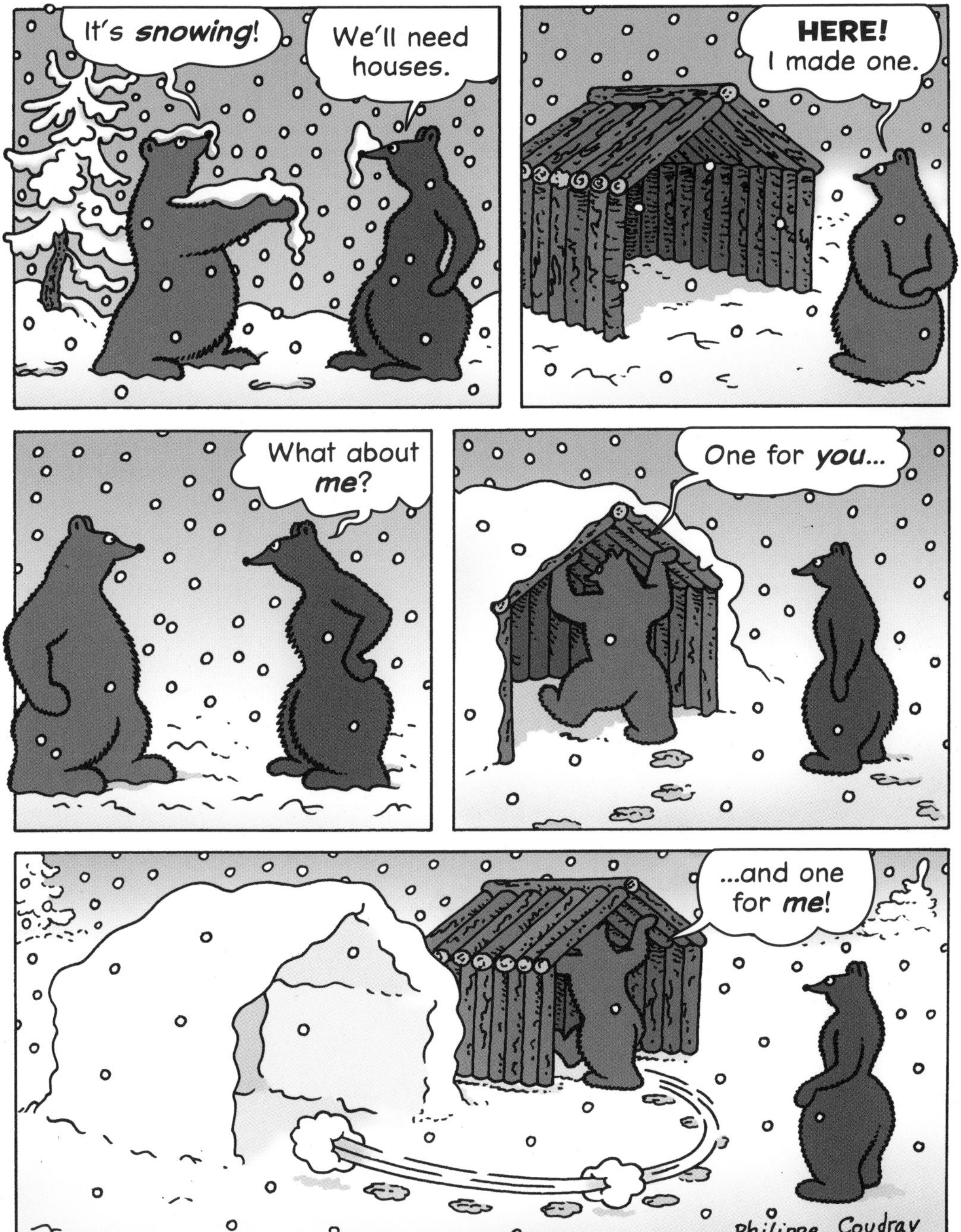
It's *snowing*!
We'll need houses.
HERE! I made one.
What about *me*?
One for *you*...
...and one for *me*!
Philippe Coudray

The house

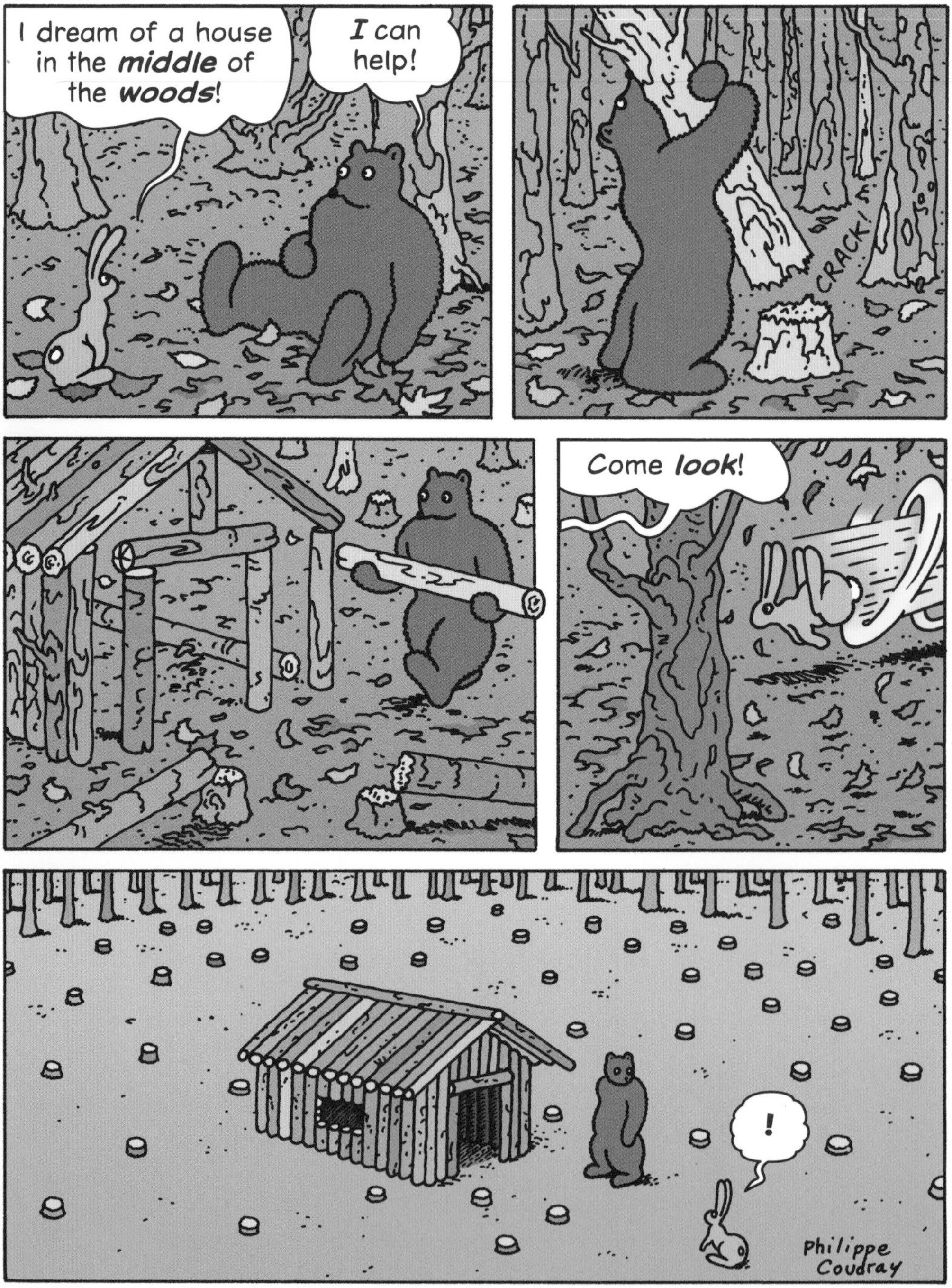
I dream of a house in the *middle* of the *woods*!
I can help!
CRACK!
Come *look*!
!
Philippe Coudray

Air mail

Philippe Coudray

25

Ringleader

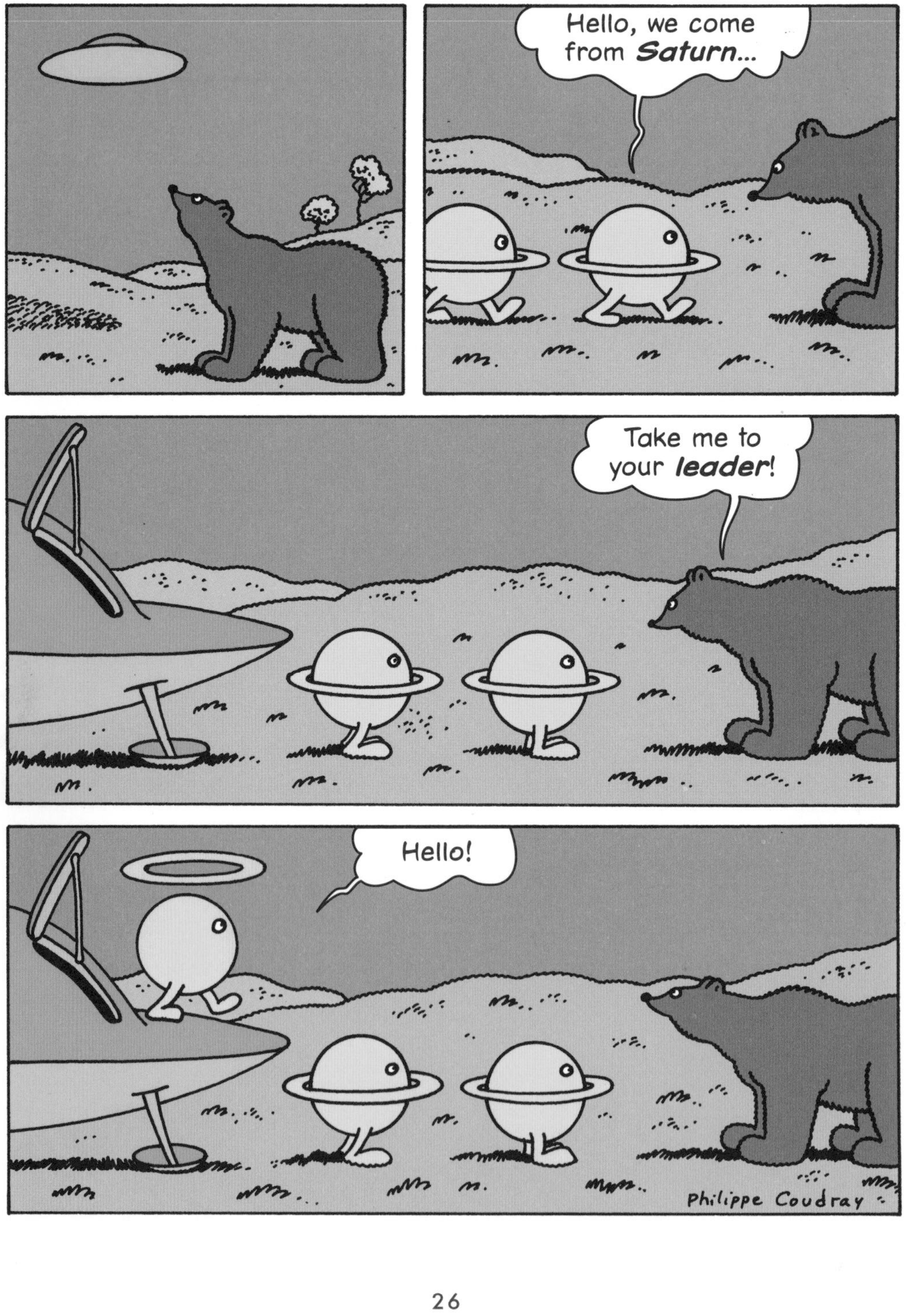
Hello, we come from Saturn...
Take me to your leader!
Hello!
Philippe Coudray

Reflection

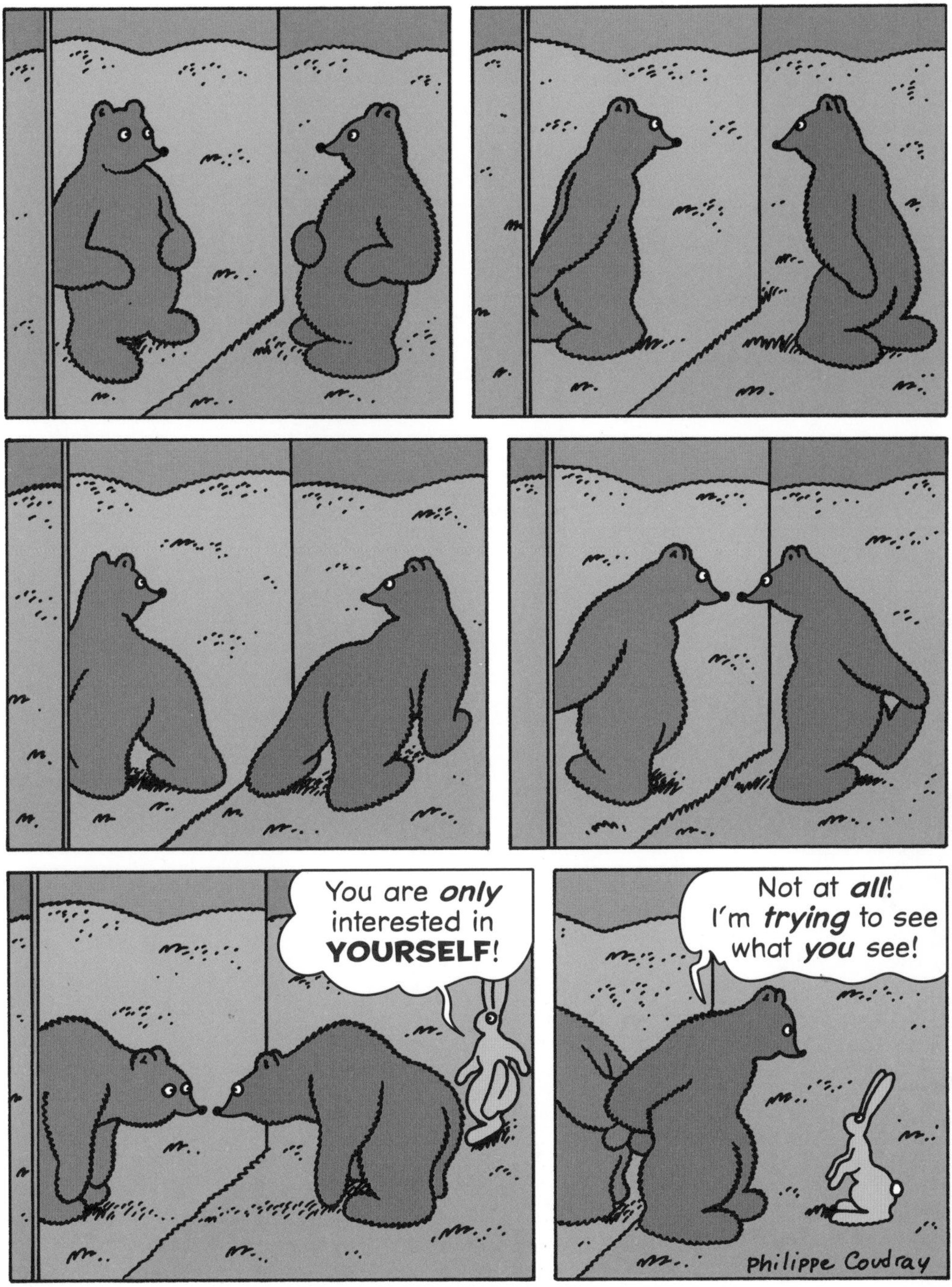
You are *only* interested in **YOURSELF**!
Not at *all*! I'm *trying* to see what *you* see!
Philippe Coudray

All tied up

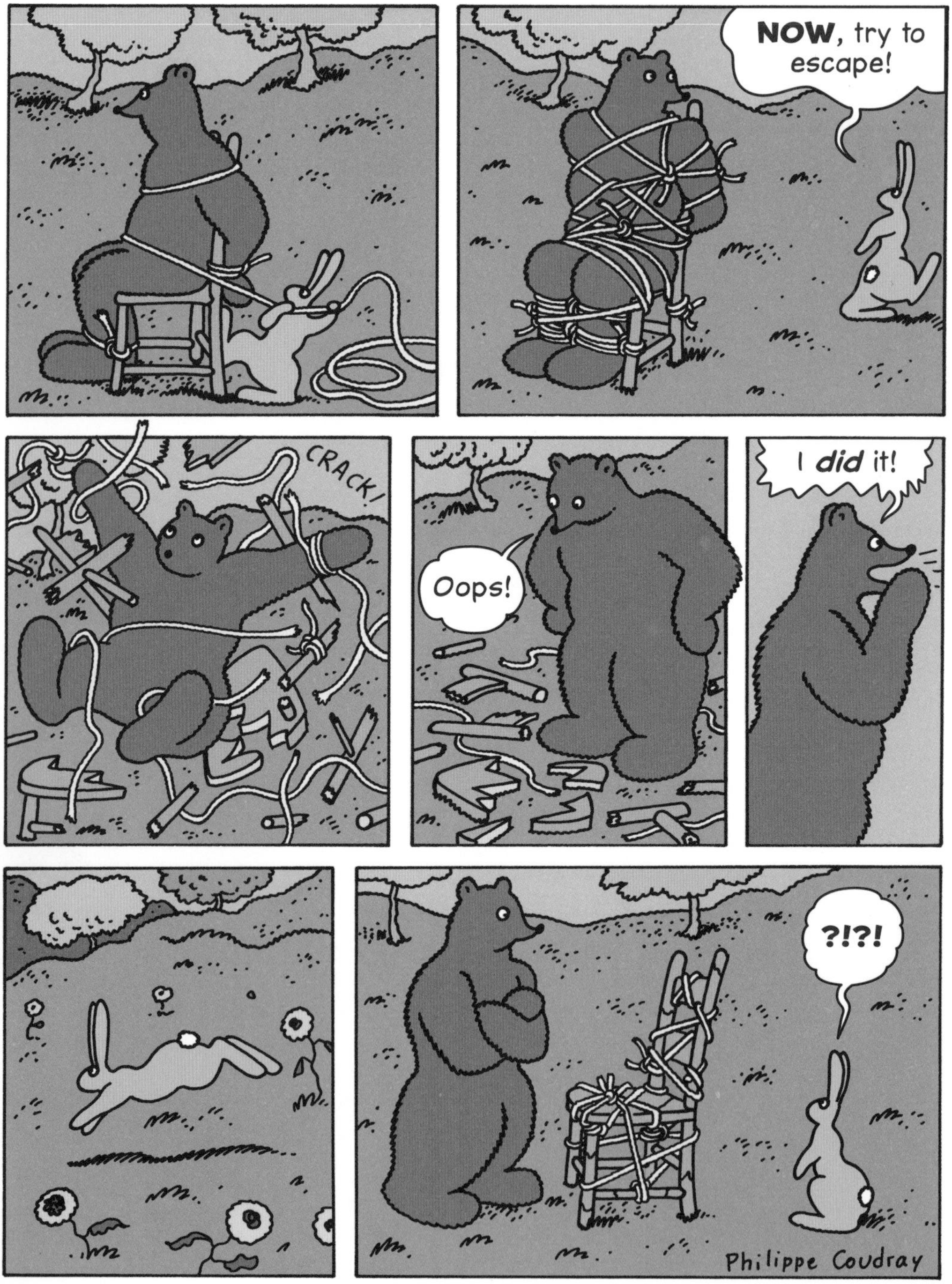

NOW, try to escape!
CRACK!
Oops!
I *did* it!
?!?!
Philippe Coudray

A gift for you

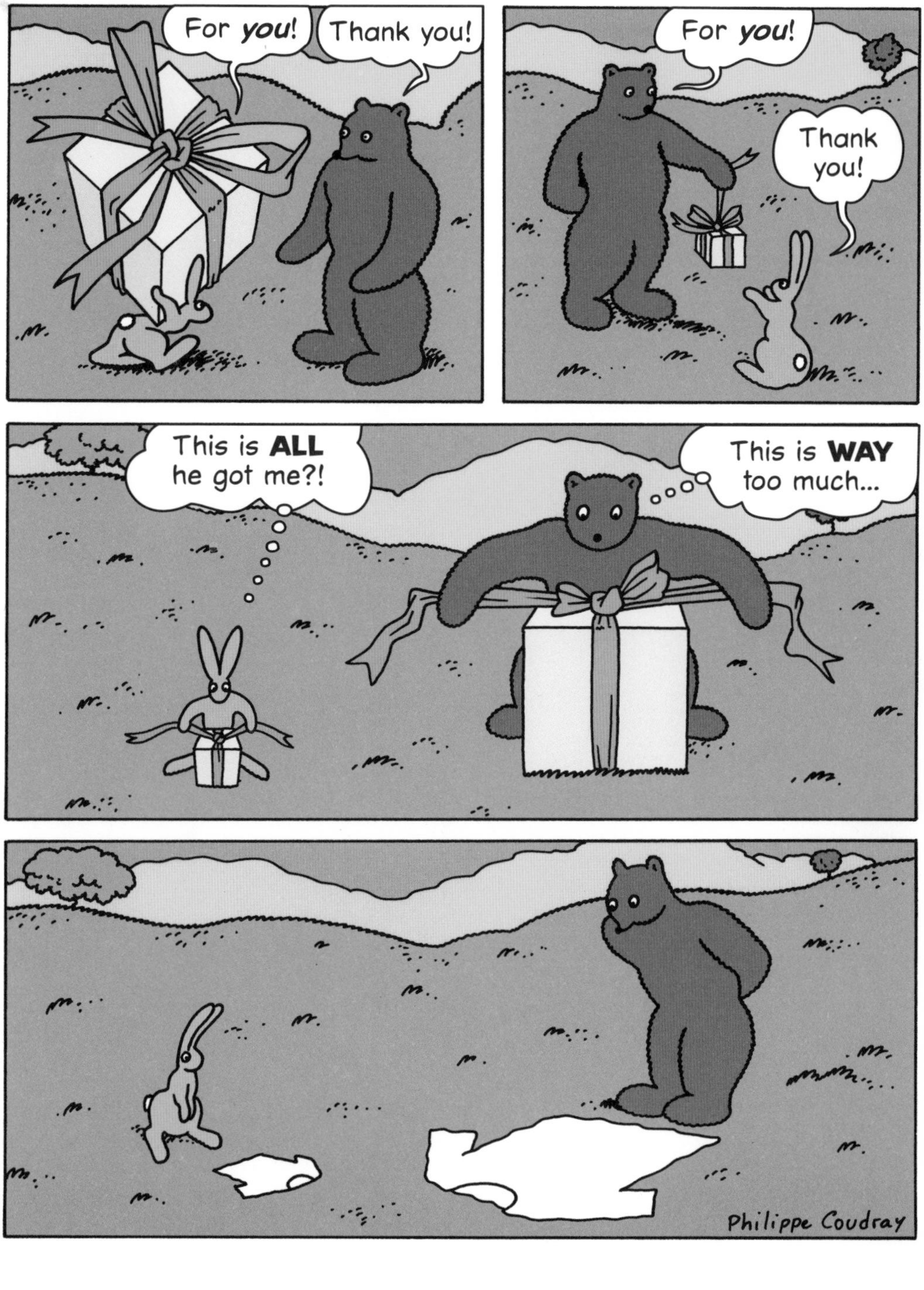
For *you*!
Thank you!
For *you*!
Thank you!
This is **ALL** he got me?!
This is **WAY** too much...
Philippe Coudray

Bird-watching

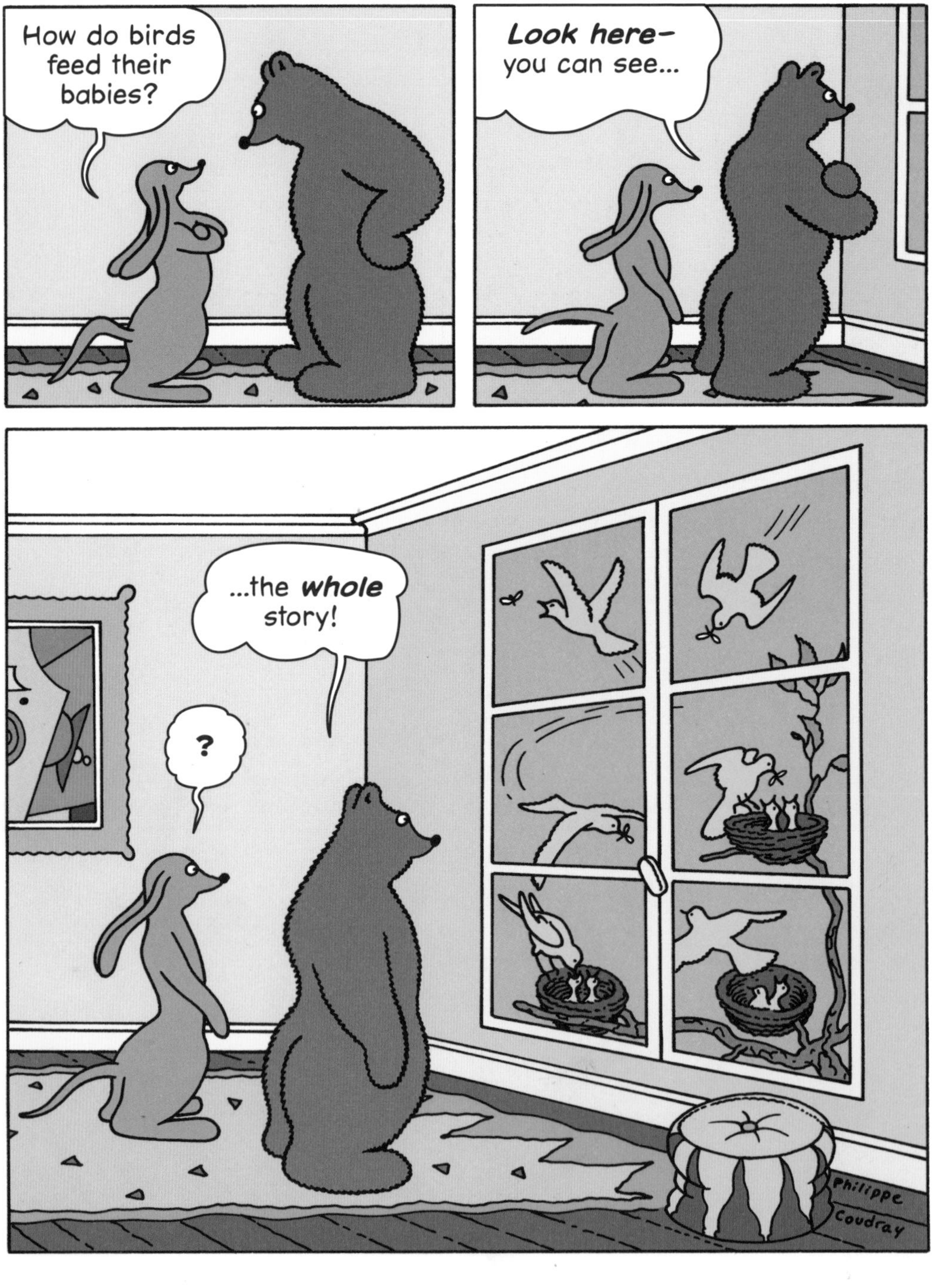
How do birds feed their babies?
Look here– you can see...
...the *whole* story!
?
Philippe Coudray

Too smart for his own good

THE END

ABOUT THE AUTHOR

PHILIPPE COUDRAY loves drawing comics and working with his twin brother Jean-Luc, who is also a humorist. Philippe's books are often used in the schools of France, his home country, where Benjamin Bear's French cousin, Barnabé, has won many prizes. In the U.S., *Benjamin Bear in Fuzzy Thinking* was nominated for an Eisner Award.

When he was younger, Philippe spent many of his family vacations in the mountains. He says, "I wanted to write a story about a bear because I love drawing the mountains where they live." In addition to his annual trip to Canada in search of Bigfoot, he enjoys creating stereoscopic images, and researching mythical creatures and other strange beasts.

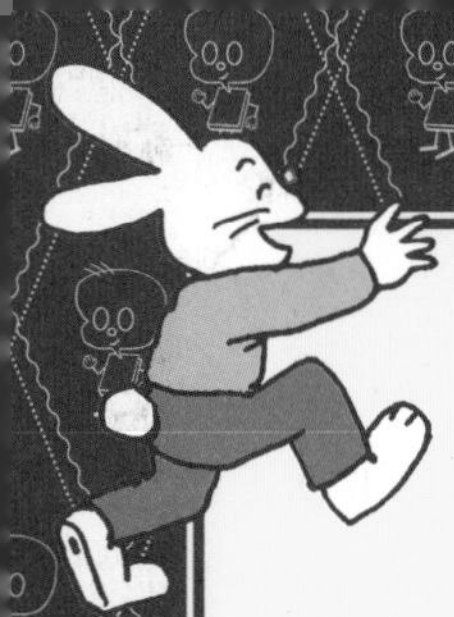

TIPS FOR PARENTS AND TEACHERS:

HOW TO READ COMICS WITH KIDS

Kids **love** comics! They are naturally drawn to the details in the pictures, which make them want to read the words. Comics beg for repeated readings and let both emerging and reluctant readers enjoy complex stories with a rich vocabulary. But since comics have their own grammar, here are a few tips for reading them with kids:

GUIDE YOUNG READERS: Use your finger to show your place in the text, but keep it at the bottom of the speaking character so it doesn't hide the very important facial expressions.

HAM IT UP! Think of the comic book story as a play and don't hesitate to read with expression and intonation. Assign parts or get kids to supply the sound effects, a great way to reinforce phonics skills.

LET THEM GUESS. Comics provide lots of context for the words, so emerging readers can make informed guesses. Like jigsaw puzzles, comics ask readers to make connections, so check a young audience's understanding by asking "What's this character thinking?" (but don't be surprised if a kid finds some of the comics' subtle details faster than you).

TALK ABOUT THE PICTURES. Point out how the artist paces the story with pauses (silent panels) or speeded-up action (a burst of short panels). Discuss how the size and shape of the panels carry meaning.

ABOVE ALL, ENJOY! There is of course never one right way to read, so go for the shared pleasure. Once children make the story happen in their imaginations, they have discovered the thrill of reading, and you won't be able to stop them. At that point, just go get them more books, and more comics.

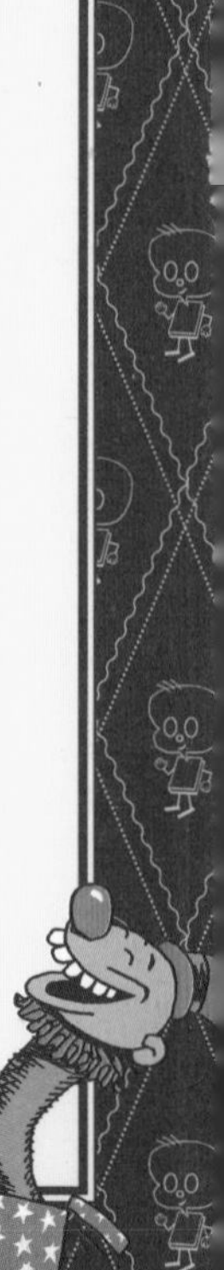